MW01078038

Little People, BIG DREAMS™

KATHERINE JOHNSON

Written by
Maria Isabel Sánchez Vegara

Illustrated by
Jemma Skidmore

Frances Lincoln
Children's Books

Once, in West Virginia, lived a Black girl
named Katherine who loved numbers.

From sunrise to sunset, she counted the clouds in the sky, the pages in books, the steps to the road . . . anything there was to count!

She got her talent for math from her dad, who could quickly add, subtract, and do difficult arithmetic in his head.

Sadly, he had to leave school when he was only twelve, but Katherine hoped that her story would be different.

Katherine worked so hard that she was ready to start high school four years early.

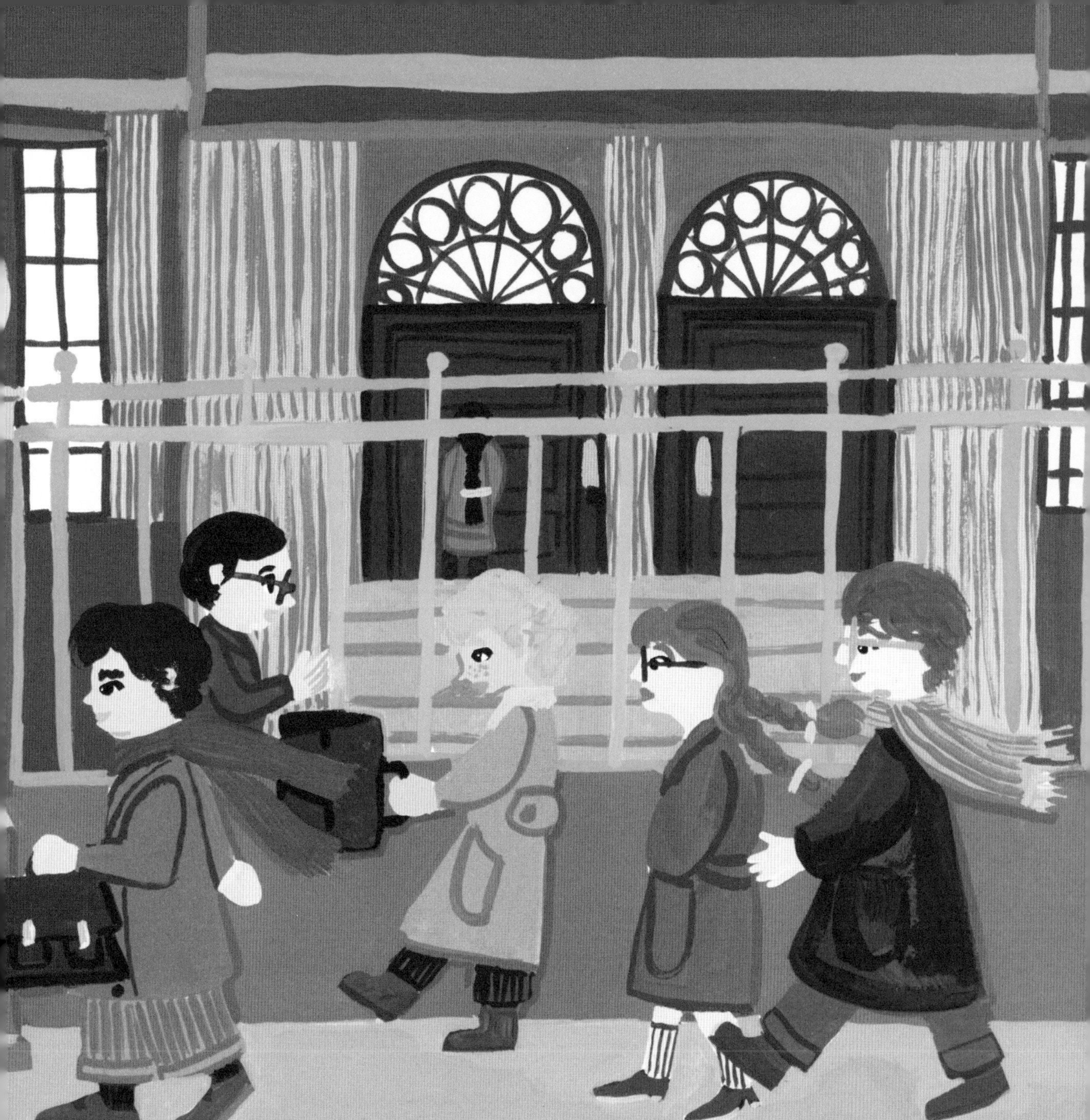

Yet, where she lived, the people in charge decided that only white students could go to the public high schools.

Determined to give their children the education they deserved, her parents moved the family to a town 120 miles away.

Here, Katherine could continue her studies. She was just fourteen when she received her high school diploma!

In college, Katherine studied French and math and graduated with honors. Next, she became the first Black woman to go to the top university in West Virginia.

Until then, the racist laws of the time had banned Black students from attending.

The following year, Katherine became a mom. Soon, she had three daughters to share her love of learning with.

Later, as a teacher, she taught her students
that math is all around us.

One day, Katherine was offered her dream job:
doing the calculations for airplane missions.

There, she worked with a team of brilliant Black women. They were so skilled that people called them "human computers."

Not long after, Katherine was sent to another department. Her task was to review the calculations made by the engineers. If there was a mistake, they could be sure she would find it!

At first they were shocked that a woman of color was correcting their work. But she soon proved she belonged.

When the U.S. government decided to build rockets to explore space, they needed experts like Katherine to help. Her team became part of a new space agency called NASA.

Katherine went from checking reports to writing them. She was the first woman in her department to have her name on a research paper!

Katherine also calculated the flight path of the second astronaut in space.

And when the first American circled Earth, she worked hard to make sure that he returned home safely.

Her proudest moment was when Neil Armstrong became the first person to walk on the Moon. Her calculations helped the spacecraft land successfully.

For seventeen years she kept working on plans
for new missions, including one to Mars!

Katherine was a great-grandmother by the time her extraordinary achievements were recognized.

She received the Presidential Medal of Freedom, her country's highest honor outside the military.

So, through hard work and determination, the girl who loved to count became part of the history of space exploration.

For, as little Katherine knew well: when you find what you love to do, you must give it your all.

KATHERINE JOHNSON

(Born 1918 – Died 2020)

1955

1962

From an early age, Katherine Johnson was fascinated by numbers and loved to learn. At school, math came easily to her and by age eighteen she had earned a university degree. Later, she attended graduate school at West Virginia University—the first Black female student to do so—before leaving to start a family. In 1953, Katherine took a job at the National Advisory Committee for Aeronautics (NACA), where she spent her first years checking the calculations for flight tests. She was a Black woman in a department of white male engineers, but Katherine knew her worth and refused to be held back by the gender and racial barriers of the time. She pushed her way into meetings, asked questions, and challenged mistakes, proving herself to be an essential member of the team. After the Soviet

1980

2015

Union launched the first satellite into space in 1957, the United States accelerated its own space program. NACA transformed into America's space agency, NASA, and Katherine's department was center-stage. It was Katherine who calculated the flight path of the first American in space, Alan Shepard, in 1961. The following year, astronaut John Glenn insisted that she personally check the computer calculations for his daring orbit around Earth. When humans landed on the Moon in 1969, Katherine was part of the team that got them there. She worked on many other space missions before she retired. It was only years later, when she was in her 90s, that her incredible achievements became widely known. Today, her life continues to inspire, reminding us to believe in ourselves and do what we love.

Want to find out more about **Katherine Johnson**?

Have a read of these great books:

Hidden Figures: The True Story of Four Black Women and the Space Race
by Margot Lee Shetterly and Laura Freeman

Counting on Katherine: How Katherine Johnson Saved Apollo 13
by Helaine Becker and Dow Phumiruk

Text © 2025 Maria Isabel Sánchez Vegara. Illustrations © 2025 Jemma Skidmore.
Original idea of the series by Maria Isabel Sánchez Vegara, published by Alba Editorial, s.l.u.
"Little People, BIG DREAMS" and "Pequeña & Grande" are trademarks of
Alba Editorial s.l.u. and/or Beautifool Couple S.L.
First published in the US in 2025 by Frances Lincoln Children's Books, an imprint of The Quarto Group.
Quarto Boston North Shore, 100 Cummings Center, Suite 265D, Beverly, MA 01915, USA
Tel: +1 978-282-9590 **www.Quarto.com**

No part of this publication may be reproduced, stored in a retrieval system, or transmitted, in any form, or by any means, electrical, mechanical, photocopying, recording, or otherwise without the prior written permission of the publisher or a license permitting restricted copying.

This book is not authorized, licensed, or approved by the estate of Katherine Johnson.
Any faults are the publisher's who will be happy to rectify for future printings.
A CIP record for this book is available from the Library of Congress.
ISBN 978-1-83600-177-5
Set in Futura BT.

Published by Peter Marley · Edited by Molly Mead
Designed by Sasha Moxon and Izzy Bowman
Production by Robin Boothroyd
Manufactured in Guangdong, China CC092024
1 3 5 7 9 8 6 4 2

Photographic acknowledgments (pages 28-29, from left to right): 1. Portrait of Katherine Johnson, a female physicist and scientist for NASA/NACA, 1955. Image courtesy of NASA © Smith Collection/Gado/Contributor/Archive Photos via Getty Images. 2. Katherine Johnson At Work, NASA space scientist and mathematician Katherine Johnson poses for a portrait at her desk with an adding machine and a 'Celestial Training device' at NASA Langley Research Center in 1962 in Hampton, Virginia © NASA/Donaldson Collection/Contributor/Michael Ochs Archives via Getty Images. 3. African American Mathematician Katherine Johnson, working at NASA's Langley Research Center in 1980 © HUM Images/Contributor/Universal Images Group Editorial via Getty Images. 4. 2015 Presidential Medal of Freedom Ceremony: President Barack Obama presents Katherine G. Johnson with the Presidential Medal of Freedom during the 2015 Presidential Medal of Freedom Ceremony at the White House on November 24, 2015 in Washington, D.C. © Kris Connor/Contributor/WireImage via Getty Images.

FSC
www.fsc.org
MIX
Paper | Supporting responsible forestry
FSC® C008047

Collect the *Little People,* **BIG DREAMS**™ series:

FRIDA KAHLO · COCO CHANEL · MAYA ANGELOU · AMELIA EARHART · AGATHA CHRISTIE · MARIE CURIE · ROSA PARKS · AUDREY HEPBURN · EMMELINE PANKHURST

ELLA FITZGERALD · ADA LOVELACE · JANE AUSTEN · GEORGIA O'KEEFFE · HARRIET TUBMAN · ANNE FRANK · MOTHER TERESA · JOSEPHINE BAKER · L. M. MONTGOMERY

JANE GOODALL · SIMONE DE BEAUVOIR · MUHAMMAD ALI · STEPHEN HAWKING · MARIA MONTESSORI · VIVIENNE WESTWOOD · MAHATMA GANDHI · DAVID BOWIE · WILMA RUDOLPH

DOLLY PARTON · BRUCE LEE · RUDOLF NUREYEV · ZAHA HADID · MARY SHELLEY · MARTIN LUTHER KING JR. · DAVID ATTENBOROUGH · ASTRID LINDGREN · EVONNE GOOLAGONG

BOB DYLAN · ALAN TURING · BILLIE JEAN KING · GRETA THUNBERG · JESSE OWENS · JEAN-MICHEL BASQUIAT · ARETHA FRANKLIN · CORAZON AQUINO · PELÉ

ERNEST SHACKLETON · STEVE JOBS · AYRTON SENNA · LOUISE BOURGEOIS · ELTON JOHN · JOHN LENNON · PRINCE · CHARLES DARWIN · CAPTAIN TOM MOORE

HANS CHRISTIAN ANDERSEN · STEVIE WONDER · MEGAN RAPINOE · MARY ANNING · MALALA YOUSAFZAI · ANDY WARHOL · RUPAUL · MICHELLE OBAMA · MINDY KALING

IRIS APFEL · ROSALIND FRANKLIN · RUTH BADER GINSBURG · MARILYN MONROE · KAMALA HARRIS · ALBERT EINSTEIN · CHARLES DICKENS · YOKO ONO · MICHAEL JORDAN

NELSON MANDELA | PABLO PICASSO | AMANDA GORMAN | GLORIA STEINEM | FLORENCE NIGHTINGALE | HARRY HOUDINI | J.R.R. TOLKIEN | ELVIS PRESLEY | NEIL ARMSTRONG

ALEXANDER VON HUMBOLDT | NIKOLA TESLA | WILMA MANKILLER | MARCUS RASHFORD | LAVERNE COX | MAE JEMISON | DWAYNE JOHNSON | HELEN KELLER | ANNA PAVLOVA

QUEEN ELIZABETH | TERRY FOX | HEDY LAMARR | SHAKIRA | FREDDIE MERCURY | LEWIS HAMILTON | LOUIS PASTEUR | PRINCESS DIANA | DAVID HOCKNEY

VANESSA NAKATE | OLIVE MORRIS | KING CHARLES | MOZART | STEVE IRWIN | JÜRGEN KLOPP | LEO MESSI | SALLY RIDE | TENZING NORGAY

KYLIE MINOGUE | BEYONCÉ | TAYLOR SWIFT | RAFA NADAL | USAIN BOLT | SIMONE BILES | STAN LEE | LEONARD COHEN | VINCENT VAN GOGH

MARY KOM | SALVADOR DALÍ | ANTOINE DE SAINT-EXUPÉRY | DAVID BECKHAM | KATHERINE JOHNSON | YAYOI KUSAMA

Scan the QR code for free activity sheets, teachers' notes and more information about the series at www.littlepeoplebigdreams.com

∫ de
√36 = -2
6 = 2
2 = 2
(x² - 6x + 8)